The Dog Detectives in...
Lost in London

illustrated by Monika Suska

The Dog Detectives are cycling through the busy
streets of London when they crash into a new case.

Can you help the Dog Detectives solve the riddle of
the missing ravens?

Lost in London, what a place to be! So much to do, so much to see. History, mystery and underground trains, giant red buses and cobblestone lanes.

Amid the whizz and the whirr of the busy old streets, animals scurry, flutter and sleep. The most famous of all are kept in a tower... Six black ravens with mystical powers.

There is a legend that says the ravens must stay or the Tower of London will crumble and the kingdom decay.

The six ravens were watching the sun set over London when a bat swooped down from above.

"You look bored," he said. "Want to play hide-and-seek?"

"That sounds fun," replied Thor, the loudest raven of all, "but we're not allowed to leave the tower."

"Don't worry," said the bat. "I promise to find you all before bedtime. I'll start counting. 1,2,3..."

The next morning the Dog Detectives, Detective Jack and Deputy Poco Loco, were a fox trot away when...

"HALT!" a police officer shouted. Detective Jack swerved and tumbled into a newspaper stand.

London is doomed," cried the officer. "We must find the ravens!"
"Fear not," said Detective Jack. "We'll have this case wrapped up
n time for afternoon tea. You can bet your biscuits on it."

They raced along the River Thames to the London Eye.

"Top of the morning to you," came a voice from the ticket desk.
"I am the Rat Riddler, the eyes and ears of the city."
"Do you know about the missing ravens?" asked Detective Jack.

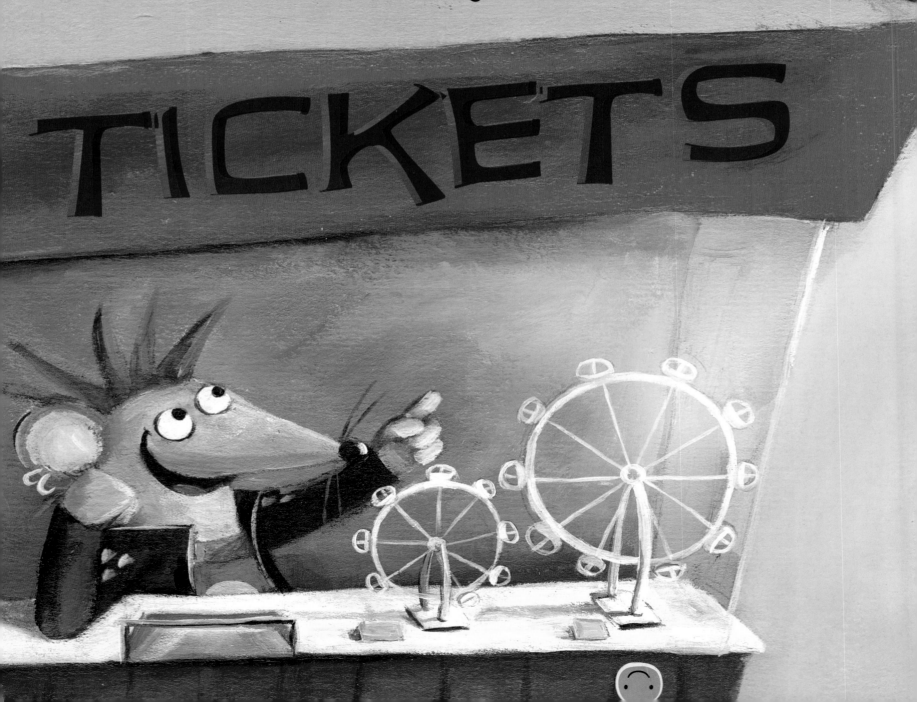

"Like a genie I'll give you three clues," said the Rat Riddler. "Clue number one... *I have a face and two hands but cannot walk. I count to twelve but cannot talk. What am I?*"

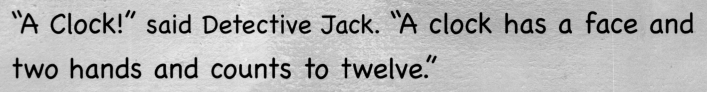

"A Clock!" said Detective Jack. "A clock has a face and two hands and counts to twelve."

"Your answer is right on time," said the Rat Riddler.

They jumped on a bus and headed towards Big Ben, the biggest clock tower of all. The Dog Detectives looked up and found the first missing raven.

"Now for clue number two," said the Rat Riddler. "She wears a crown upon her head and falls asleep in a royal bed."

"That's easy," said Deputy Poco Loco wagging his tail.
"The Queen wears a crown and sleeps in a royal bed."

The team cycled to the gates of Buckingham Palace and
spotted the second missing raven.

"Smashing!" said the Rat Riddler. "And now for my final clue. *I wear bark, grow leaves and shade parks. What am I?*"

"A tree wears bark, grows leaves and shades parks,"
cried Deputy Poco Loco.

The Dog Detectives pedalled full tilt through the parks of London
until high in the treetops they saw the third missing raven.
"What better place to hide than Hyde Park," said Detective Jack.

Deputy Poco Loco scratched his ears.
"If I were a raven I'd hide somewhere
busy and loud, to be hidden away in the
bustling crowd."

The team wormed their way through giant red buses and honking black cars.

There among the clatter and chatter of Trafalgar Square was the fourth missing raven.

"Well done Deputy," said Detective Jack. "If I were a raven I'd feel right at home, nestled high up in the roof of a dome."

The team jumped back on their bikes and hot-dogged it to the biggest dome in the city. They ran up the steps of St. Paul's Cathedral and pushed open the heavy wooden doors.

Blending into the magnificent dome was the fifth missing raven.

The team circled the city in search of the final missing raven.

They found bats beneath bridges

...a spattering of sparrows

...and a family of foxes, but no raven.

Where was Thor, the loudest raven of all?

"It's almost time for afternoon tea," said Detective Jack, rubbing his belly. "Could you please give us one more clue?"

"Well I guess...I see...I do suppose," said the Rat Riddler. *"What's lost is right beneath your nose."*

The Dog Detectives knew there was one place they hadn't searched. They whizzed down into the London Underground for a shortcut across the city.

CAMDEN TOWN

There waiting patiently at the Tower of London was Thor, the last missing raven. "Looks like I'm the winner of hide-and-seek," Thor said proudly.

The Rat Riddler smiled. "Sometimes the hardest thing to find is right under your nose."

"Well, now that London is safe and sound," said Detective Jack. "Here is a riddle for all of you. *What starts with a T and ends with a T, and has T in it?*"

...A Teapot!

THE END

London Facts

London is the capital city of Great Britain, famous for its vibrant history and important landmarks. It is one of the most visited cities in the world.

There are many ways to travel around London such as the iconic red London buses, public bicycles and the underground trains.

Tower Bridge

Wish you were here!
Love
the Dog Detectives x

William K. Wombat

In a Hole

The Outback

AUSTRALIA

The Legend of the Ravens dates back hundreds of years when King Charles II made it known that at least six ravens must be kept at the Tower of London; without them Great Britain would fall.

Trafalgar Square is home to Nelson's Column, paid for by the English people to honour the victory of Admiral Nelson during the battle of Trafalgar. Today, Trafalgar Square is a meeting place, rich in art and architecture.

The Tower of London was built almost 1000 years ago. It has been a fortress, a royal palace, an armoury and a prison where beheadings took place. It is now home to the crown jewels, which are guarded by the **Yeoman Warders**, who are also known as Beefeaters.

St Paul's Cathedral has been rebuilt four times. The present one, designed by Sir Christopher Wren, was built when the old one burned down in the Great Fire. Since then the cathedral has survived World War II and the Blitz.

Tower of London

Hyde Park is the largest park in London and was orginally used by King Henry VIII for hunting. Nowadays the park is open to everyone. Its most visited sites are Speaker's Corner and the Memorial Fountain for Diana, Princess of Wales.

The London Eye was opened in the year 2000 and was originally known as the Millennium Wheel. It was built as a symbol of modern London. When in a 'capsule' at the top of the Eye you can see 40km in every direction.

Big Ben is the massive bell inside the famous clock tower of Westminster Palace. The bell is heavier than a killer whale and very loud. Big Ben rings every hour, with smaller bells riging every quarter.

Want to read more?

ISBN 978-1-84886-062-9

The Dog Detectives
by Fin & Zoa illustrated by Monika Suska
AN OUTBACK ODYSSEY

The Dog Detectives
by Fin & Zoa illustrated by Monika Suska
The Great Grizzly North

ISBN 978-1-84886-068-1

Lost in London
is an original concept by
authors Zoa & Fin

©Dawn Lumsden
Illustrated by Monika Suska
Monika Suska is represented by MSM Studio
www.msmstudio.eu

A CIP catalogue record for this book is
available at the British Library.

Maverick Arts Publishing Ltd
Studio 3A
City Business Centre
6 Brighton Road
Horsham
West Sussex
RH13 5BB
+44(0) 1403 256941

**PUBLISHED BY MAVERICK ARTS
PUBLISHING LTD**

©Maverick Arts Publishing Limited
May 2011
Reprinted October 2011
Reprinted 2014

ISBN 978-1-84886-069-8

www.maverickbooks.co.uk

THIS EDITION PUBLISHE
2014 FOR INDEX BOO